To Manuela, Zoe, Stella, Alia, Cristina, Hana, Margherita, Robin, Elia, Lola, May, Matilde, Esti, Isabella, Mili, Mar, Dima, Mayte, Alice, Juana, Coni, Lina, Ellen, Maria, Giovanna, Mariola, Teddi, Daniela, Ester, Merche, Giulia, Cecilia, Marina, Blu Jeny, Miryam, Emilie, Chela, Tiziana, Rima, Valeria, Sonja and Elena.

Dolores Brown

To Luna, my mother, Dani, Astrid, Annerose, Graciela, Maru, Fernanda, Mª Angeles, Juana Marie, Sandra, Begoña, Rebeca, Sophia, Doris, Eva, Wilma, Uschi, Gabi, Heike, Marion, Susanne, Penelopa, Vroni, Crisztina, Patricia, Ana, Rosi, Robin, to the women of my German and Argentinian family, and to all the ladies of Barcelona.

Sonja Wimmer

The Truly Brave Princesses
Egalité Series

© Text: Dolores Brown, 2018
© Illustrations: Sonja Wimmer, 2018
© Edition: NubeOcho, 2018
www.nubeocho.com - hello@nubeocho.com

Text editing: Eva Burke and Rebecca Packard

Distributed in the United States by
Consortium Book Sales & Distribution

First edition: 2018
ISBN: 978-84-17123-38-3

Printed in China by Asia Pacific Offset,
respecting international labor standards.

The Truly Brave
PRINCESSES

Dolores Brown

Sonja Wimmer

Perhaps on more than one occasion you've seen a **princess**.

Maybe you didn't realize she was actually a princess, because at that moment she was **not wearing her crown**.

But if you **open your eyes wide and your heart,**
you will discover that there are more princesses than you ever imagined.

Maybe she's a neighbor,
maybe a schoolmate,
maybe the cashier at your supermarket...
Or maybe, one day when you ride the subway, you will discover a **little princess there**.

From now on, you will realize that there are many, many princesses.

There is always one **much closer** than you think.

Name: *Princess Anita*

Age: *29 years*

Profession: *Physician*

She loves: *Running in the rain and drinking hot chocolate on cold days*

Princess Anita does not usually wait for the prince to come home; it is he who usually waits for her.

Although her hospital emergency shifts are exhausting, she always returns eagerly to work the following day.

Princess Rita has braces and a wonderful smile.

She takes part in school plays every Thursday and always laughs with joy when she receives applause.

Name: *Princess Rita*

Age: *11 years*

When she grows up she wants to be: an Actress

She loves: *Wearing a clown nose and surprising people on the street*

Nº F 136

Name: *Princess Beatrix*

Age: *43 years*

Profession: *Hairdresser*

She loves: *Wearing costumes and strolling through the forest looking for fantastical creatures*

Princess Beatrix
is a single mother.

Little Daniel is always fascinated by the special hairstyles his mother creates for him.

Sometimes they disguise themselves as pirates and find treasure.

Name: *Princess Neyla*

Age: *39 years*

Profession: *Architect*

She loves: *Scuba diving and underwater photography*

Princess Neyla designs houses to fulfill the dreams of many people.

The prince is a stay-at-home dad. He enjoys taking care of the little ones.

When Princess Neyla leaves early to go to work, her family is always there to wave goodbye.

Princess Gilda is single.

When she's working, she likes to give warm smiles to each and every customer.

Everyone loves to go through her checkout lane, even if they have to wait.

Name: Princess Gilda

Age: 53 years

Profession: Supermarket cashier

She loves: Going up to the roof at night to catch shooting stars

Princess Kristen is proud to have exactly 47 freckles.

She has a lazy eye, but her slam dunks are terrific when she plays basketball.

Name: Princess Kristen

Age: 7 years

When she grows up she wants to be: a Superheroine

She loves: Reading books about magic and climbing to the highest point of her favorite tree to see beyond the horizon

Name: Princess Robin

Age: 37 years

Profession: Librarian

She loves: Going dancing with her friends and having pillow fights with her kids

Princess Robin is divorced.

She organizes regular movie nights with her children and friends on her porch in the evenings.

In her spare time, she writes novels. Her new book is about to be published.

Name: Princess Liang

Age: 24 years

Profession: Translator

She loves: Writing colorful and exotic postcards to her friends and getting them little souvenirs. She also loves collecting maps of the ancient world

Princess Liang speaks French, German, English and Chinese.

It fascinates her to communicate in different languages. That's why she enjoys traveling so much.

She sometimes travels with her friends and other times with the prince.

Name: *Princess Alice*

Age: *29 years*

Profession: *Blogger and Graphic Designer*

She loves: *Surfing the world's craziest waves with Prince Samuel and their dog Max*

Princess Alice just got married.
Prince Samuel was planning to propose,
but she proposed first.

Name: Princess Dolores

Age: 14 years

When she grows up she wants to be: a Singer

She loves: Going to the dog shelter to help with feeding and walking the abandoned dogs. Timo is one of her favorites

Princess Dolores is very popular among her friends.

She has a very pretty voice. When she plays the guitar and sings, everyone is mesmerized.

Princess Lois is a dentist. Not a single child comes to her clinic with fear. She is married to Princess Maggie.

Princess Maggie is a mail carrier. She loves to deliver postcards from distant lands.

Name: *Princess Lois*

Age: *32 years*

Profession: *Dentist*

Name: *Princess Maggie*

Age: *27 years*

Profession: *Mail Carrier*

They love: *Creating puppet shows for children in their neighborhood*

BY AIR MAIL

Name: *Princess Agnes*

Age: *68 years*

Profession: *Retired*

She loves: *Photography. Her Instagram account has many followers. She also loves to go dancing*

Princess Agnes
is a widow.

She spends a lot of time
with her friends.

She has recently met a
prince and they go out
together frequently.

Princess Caroline has Down syndrome. She works in an office, and in her spare time she likes to play volleyball.

Princess Catori never got married, but she lives with the prince and they love each other very much.

She regards her job as very important. It makes her happy to help make the world a fairer place.

Name: Princess Catori

Age: 47 years

Profession: Lawyer

She loves: Trying the desserts that the prince prepares. Tiramisu is her favorite!

Name: *Princess Esther*

Age: *9 years*

When she grows up she wants to be: *a Journalist*

She loves: *Interviewing her colleagues and recording short videos*

Princess Esther
has a lisp, but she is not afraid to speak out and she is very good at telling jokes.

DAILY NEWS

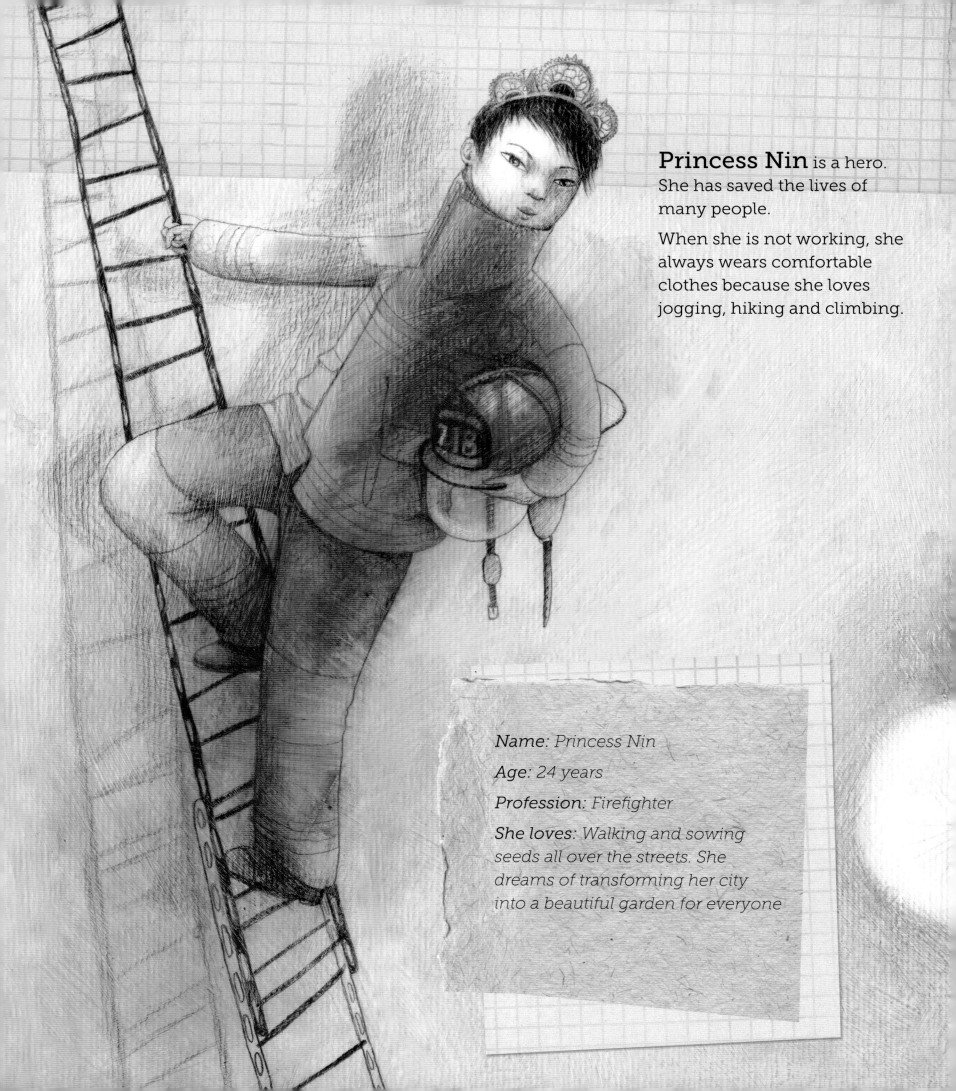

Princess Nin is a hero. She has saved the lives of many people.

When she is not working, she always wears comfortable clothes because she loves jogging, hiking and climbing.

Name: Princess Nin

Age: 24 years

Profession: Firefighter

She loves: Walking and sowing seeds all over the streets. She dreams of transforming her city into a beautiful garden for everyone

Name: *Princess Zoe*

Age: *27 years*

Profession: *Astronaut*

She loves: *Feeling closer to the stars and seeing her coffee floating around without the force of gravity*

Princess Zoe has retired her crown.

Now she travels through distant space and does not want to be a princess anymore.